The Case
of the Lost Kid:

Adventures of Charlie #2

By
Rae Lowery

PublishAmerica
Baltimore

PublishAmerica has allowed this work to remain exactly as the author intended, verbatim, without editorial input.

ISBN: 1-60703-921-4
PUBLISHED BY PUBLISHAMERICA, LLLP
www.publishamerica.com
Baltimore

Printed in the United States of America

Who Are These Guys?

Amanda—Delight's 3 year old sister.

Ashley—My other best friend.

Bethany—Jer's trendy sister.

Charlie—That's ME!

Chris Thomas—The kid in the mystery car.

Dallin—My little brother.

Danielle—Delight's baby sister.

Darric—The hottest guy at my school.

Delight—My best friend.

Jennifer—Delight's 7 year old sister.

Jer—My neighbor with the really cool truck.

John—Okay, okay, he's a boy, but he's also one of my best friends.

Jon—DIFFERENT SPELLING than my friend John. This is a kid at school that thinks he is an alien from the planet Pluto with green antennae and is 327 years old.

Lieutenant Eric Miller—The police officer that helped me.

Miss Sellwood—the librarian at my school.

Ms. Angela Krump—My teacher at school.

Polly—The lady in the gray car.

Sarah—Chris Thomas's sister.

Tiffany—A teenage girl that goes to my church.

Wade—My big brother that is off at college.

The Case of the Lost Kid:

Adventures of Charlie #2

Chapter One

Okay, here's the deal.

I only wanted to go to the store and get some gum. Just a simple bike ride that would change my life forever.

Let me back up. My name is Charlie, and I am 11 years old. People tell me I am a tomboy, but I just think of myself as a regular kid. I do like spiders though. And climbing trees. And going on adventures. Plus, I collect words. When I hear a word I've never heard of, I try really hard to remember it until I can get to a dictionary and find out what it means. I will save you the trouble of having to do that because when I use one of my spectacular words I will tell you what it means at the bottom of the page.

Anyhoo, my mom was kind of getting on my last nerve so I wanted to get out of the house and get some gum. Sometimes it helps to put a huge wad of gum in your mouth and chew away your stress. I got on my bike and rode to the corner, and I was just about to cross the street when I saw a kid in the back seat of a long gray car. That wasn't odd by itself, but, I don't know, just something in the way that kid looked at me made me stare at him. It was like his eyes were telling me he needed help or something. I looked at the license plate on the car and told myself to remember it. KNH831.

I tried to think of a sentence or a word that used those letters. Then I thought of "kid needs help" and made a face out of the 831 by mentally turning it sideways and making the 8 eyes, the 3 a nose, and the 1 a mouth. Pretty cool, huh?

When I got to the store, I got my favorite gum. Well, actually, they were out of the kind I like the best, so I got my second most favorite, which is the kind that is all rolled up like a tape measure. I call it tapeworm gum because in school we learned about tapeworms that live inside people and eat all their food from the INSIDE of their bodies and then the people get really skinny, and it's pretty sick but hey, nature has her own rules, no matter how disgusting.

Anyhoo, I asked the clerk if I could use his pen to write down the license plate of this car just in case I forgot the numbers. While I was riding back, I saw my friend Delight. She was on her way home to watch her baby sister, who is just learning to walk. That's not so bad, except that the baby can walk well enough to get into stuff now, so she will crash around the room until she finds a table that is low enough for her to grab onto, and she will pull everything down onto the floor. Then, she eats it. I'm not just talking about paper either. She eats rubber bands, pencils, aluminum foil, dead insects, you name it. Her name is Danielle. It's a very cute name, but don't let it fool you. The child is an animal.

Delight's dad is a cop, so I thought he might have some way to find out about what kind of a person owned the gray car. I know it seems like a lot of trouble to go through to find out if this kid I had never even seen before was in trouble, but you have to understand that I am a sleuth. This kind of thing makes me feel like I have supercharged brainpower. I call it turbo-thinking.

Anyhoo, I told Delight about the situation, and she said she would talk to her dad to see if he could help. Since I didn't have anything going on at home, I just followed her home. When we got there, her mom was in the kitchen listening to her radio guru, Dr. Laurel. Since Delight's mom home schools Jennifer (the 7 year old) and Amanda (the 3 year old), she is constantly listening to Dr. Laurel to find out how to fix it when she does something horribly wrong in the parenting, schooling, or marriage department.

I asked her if I should turn up the radio, since it was hard to hear over the vacuum cleaner, which she was using to clean the countertops. Let me explain. Her mom has an unusual way of doing things. She told me she likes to vacuum the countertops because if there is something gross and sticky she doesn't have to touch it. I think she just does it because it's fun to suck things into a vacuum cleaner.

We told her mom about the kid in the car. Well, I should say we TRIED to tell her about it. Every time we started talking about it Amanda, the three year old, would do something obnoxious and distract her mom. For example, I started to tell her about seeing the look in the kid's eye, when Amanda pulled a chair into the kitchen and stood up on the countertop. When her mom told her to get down, she jumped. Onto the refrigerator. When we finally got her down from there, I started over. When I got to the part about the license plate, we heard the baby crying. Amanda was riding her like a horse while Danielle tried to crawl away. By the time I finished explaining everything, Amanda was feeding little pieces of carpet to the baby, and I gave up.

Anyway, it was time for Jennifer to go on her weekly field trip to places wild and unknown. Actually, just between you and me, I think it would be a lot of fun to have school at home and go on all those field trips. One time her math assignment was to spend 20 dollars on six different items, and make sure the correct change was given. That's a lot of brainwork for a 7 year old, but I thought it was pretty cool. Even though Jennifer is only 7, that kid is smarter than half the kids in MY class at school. I've actually had her help me with my homework before. You think she is just this sweet little kid playing with her dolls, and then you realize she is a model of our governmental system with Barbie and all her friends.

Anyhoo, since Delight's mom was leaving, I left too. Hey, nobody is gonna catch me babysitting some kamikaze kid.

Chapter Two

I decided to call the Department of Motor Vehicles and ask who owned the car. I figured if I could find out the driver's name, maybe I could find out what part of town the kid lived in and then I could see if it was someone from my school, since the car had been in my neighborhood. BAD IDEA.

Right off the bat, I could tell the lady from DMV wasn't going to help me. I don't know what it is with some grown-ups, but they really need to chill when they are dealing with kids. As soon as she answered the phone, I politely asked her the name of the person who owned a gray car with the license plate KNH831, and she said "I can't give you any information unless you own the car. Are you the car owner?"

DUH! If I owned the car, why would I be calling to ask who the owner was? I explained exactly what had happened, and told her my concerns, and she said I would have to call the police and have them contact her in order to get that information. Then, she asked me my name. In and of itself, it's not bad when someone asks you your name, but the way she said it was really rude and it gave me the feeling she was going to try to get me in trouble somehow, so I just hung up. Hey, I get in enough trouble on my own.

I waited until 4:30, and then called Delight's house. I knew her dad would be home from work by then, and in fact, he was the one that answered the phone. Unfortunately, there are rules keeping cops from just calling up the DMV and snooping around about someone unless there is something wrong. Since I really didn't have any proof that there was a problem, I just thanked him and hung up. Strike two.

While I was sitting there thinking, my little brother came in the room. His name is Dallin, and he's a pretty decent kid as six-year olds go, but sometimes he can be SO ANNOYING!!!!! He thinks it's really funny to say everything I say. I don't know why he finds this so fascinating, but sometimes, for no apparent reason, he will take a drink at the same time I do, clear his throat when I do, pick up his fork and eat a piece of the same food on his plate that I eat on mine, or whatever. When I complain, he just puts on his little angel face and my mom tells me to ignore it. Or worse, she tells me he's not doing it. I think sometimes moms forget how it is to be a kid and have a brother that drives you so crazy you just want to scream.

Anyhoo, Dallin was apparently in a good mood today, because when he walked by me, he didn't make any disgusting sounds or cross his eyes at me or pretend his hand was a tarantula running across my arm. He just smiled sweetly and walked into the other room. See, now that I said what an obnoxious child he is he just acts like he's a normal kid and no one would ever believe he could drive a person crazy. Sheesh.

I heard him in the living room playing with his mini cars, and then I got an idea. Since I had seen the mystery car in my own neighborhood once before, maybe if I rode around I could find it again. Even though it was warm outside, I grabbed a jacket so when dusk fell I wouldn't get cold. I pride myself on thinking ahead about things.

I popped some fresh gum in my mouth and jumped on my bike. It's funny how much better a person can think with a wad of gum to chomp on.

I rode for about six blocks when I saw a gray car coming toward me. I got so excited I forgot to look back down at the road, and my bike tire skidded up against the curb. It almost flipped me over, but I caught it in time. When I looked back up again, the car was turning the corner, but I could see it was a lot shorter than the one I was looking for. I had been looking so intently at the kid's face I didn't think to see what kind of a car it was, just that it was long and gray.

I rode around for about 3 hours and my legs were getting sore. I was warm from all that exercise even though it was getting chilly out. Plus, my stomach was starting to growl, so I turned around and started for home.

And then, I saw it.

Chapter Three

Ironically, I was so focused on my hungry stomach I probably wouldn't have even seen it if another car hadn't honked and made me look over at the mall. A car that looked just like the gray one was kind of circling around looking for a parking spot. There aren't enough spaces for all the cars that want to go to the mall, so we call the cars looking for spots "vultures" because sometimes they circle around 8 or 10 times before they find an opening.

I forgot all about how tired my legs were and poured on the speed to get across the street before a mass of cars blocked me from crossing. As I got closer, I could clearly see the license plate. QXR558. Rats. It was the wrong car. But the possibility that it MIGHT have been the right one gave me some energy and I was deep in thought while I pedaled home.

When I walked in the front door, my mom was in the kitchen making some Ugly Tuna. We call it that because the first time you look at it you think, "There is no way I am eating that disgusting mess." But since you'll get in BIG trouble if you actually say that (moms are funny that way) you just pretend to have a stomachache and go to your room and eat some of the chips you have stashed under the bed. The funniest part is that I wouldn't eat it until one time when we were having Ugly Tuna my dad said if I didn't eat dinner with the family I would be GROUNDED. Can you believe it? So I sat down at the table and took a bite of the stuff and it was absolutely delicious. But I still had to look across the room while I ate it. Hey, just because it tasted good didn't make it less ugly.

Anyhoo, I was starving, so I would have eaten a moldy shoe if that's what she'd been making. But I was really glad it was something delicious, because it is much funner to eat when you are really hungry. Have you ever noticed how much better food tastes if you are ravenous? By the time the food was done I was ready to eat the table.

At dinner I continued to think about what had been going through my mind on the bike ride home. Something just didn't seem right, and I couldn't put my finger on what it was. I knew there was something that looked odd about the kid other than his expression. It had been such a fleeting glance I am surprised I remember any details at all. I went over the whole thing in my head, trying to put it into slow motion.

I had been stopped at a crosswalk when I saw the car enter the intersection. The driver had looked like a chauffeur or something, because he was wearing a little cap with a dark bill that had some kind of a gold emblem on the front. He was wearing a dark jacket, even though it had been too warm outside to be wearing more than a tee-shirt.

As the car had rounded the corner, I remember wondering if there was a celebrity inside, because it looked kind of like a limo with the driver in uniform like that, and it was a long gray car. That was probably the reason I had peered inside the window the way I did. I saw a kid with a pair of brown shorts and a striped green, white, and brown polo shirt. Since I was up on the sidewalk, I could see all the way inside, and it looked like he had something in his hand. The car was waiting for traffic before it could turn, so it was a minute before it started moving again. Just as the car pulled forward, the kid noticed me looking at him. This was the weird part that got me to thinking. Instead of smiling, or frowning, or turning away, or making a face, or doing any of the zillions of things a kid does when they see someone looking at them through a car window, he did something really odd. HE FROZE. I swear, he didn't move a muscle. Like he thought I was going to hurt him somehow. It reminded me of when you turn a corner at night and an animal is in the road. And then, when the car was almost past me, it was like he realized he could somehow communicate with me and his expression went from fearful to....I don't know, just PLEADING. Like he wanted me to help him, but he still just sat there frozen. I don't know if I can explain it.

I know there was something else about it that was out of place too, but I can't put my finger on it.

My parents were talking about a problem Dallin was having at school—something about eating a goldfish, so they didn't notice how quiet I was, and I was able to just slip out of the room. When I got upstairs to my room, I closed the door and turned on my favorite CD. It's funny how music can help you feel better. I didn't want something loud and obnoxious, because it's kind of hard for me to think when I listen to that kind of music—I get too wrapped up in the beat and forget all about whatever I was trying to figure out. I decided to put on a CD I got for my birthday last year—kind of funky soft instruments and raindrops and stuff. You know, thinking music.

I laid on my bed and stared at the stars on my ceiling. Man, you should see my ceiling. It is really cool. A couple of years ago we were studying about the stars and constellations and I thought it would be really perfect to have them on my ceiling in correct order. So I bought some dark blue paint, and a small can of glow-in-the-dark paint, and took my textbook home with me. I talked my parents into letting me TRY to duplicate the picture in the book, and convinced them it would help me with my schoolwork (parents are suckers for that line) so they said yes. So now, I can just close the curtains and turn off the light and I feel like I am outside camping under the stars.

Anyhoo, I was laying there on my bed looking at the stars on my ceiling, when it hit me. I was so surprised I bolted upright in bed. I had figured out what was wrong.

Chapter Four

I ran down the stairs to ask my mom if I could go to Delight's house. It was already almost 7 pm so I wasn't upset when she said no, but I HAD to talk to someone. My other best friend Ashley was at her grandma's house for a week so I couldn't go next door and talk to her. I just had to do something. I went to the backyard and sat on my old swing set. Before I realized it, I was swinging as high as I could, wondering if something this casual was enough proof to take to an adult. Grown-ups are funny that way—they don't believe you when you say something is REALLY wrong if you can't prove it somehow. They don't usually think a gut feeling is enough. Well, this was more than just a gut feeling.

I reflected back on what I had discovered. The kid had been in an expensive car, wearing expensive clothes, with a paid driver. But the thing that was bothering me, was his HAIRCUT. It looked kind of like the time Ashley and I had tried to give her dog a trim because she had one of those tiny dogs that looks like it has droopy eyebrows and a mustache. He was perfectly happy to cooperate until he heard the scissors right by his ear, and then he bolted and hid under the couch. You can bet we had a fun time explaining to her mom why he looked like his eyebrows had been caught in a fan.

Anyhoo, the kid's bangs weren't cut straight, and the back kind of sloped up instead of being cut across all the same length. As if he were being kidnapped or something and he couldn't be taken out in public to a barber! That had to be it! That was probably why he looked so paranoid and then why he looked at me in that way that asked me to help. Now I just had to find out where he was.

Chapter Five

The next morning, I went to school early and spent a few minutes in the library. I wanted to look through all the yearbooks of the past four years to see if the kid had ever gone to my school. I kept coming back to the thought that he was in this neighborhood for a reason, and I wanted to know what it was. I knew that his picture would probably look different, but you can still tell what a person would look like last year or the year before if they don't look all that different. I pretty much look just like I did 3 years ago, but my cousin Francine used to be really cute when she was a kid, and then she hit puberty and shot up a foot in one year and got a ton of zits and her head looked too small for her nose all of a sudden. It was unfortunate that her name was Francine, because the kids started calling her Frankie—as in FRANKENSTEIN. So you can see why I hoped this kid hadn't changed since his last photo.

While I was shuffling through the pages, I saw a familiar face. TIFFANY! I forgot she had gone to this school when she was younger. Tiffany is a girl at church that always says hi to me in the halls. At first I was kind of wondering why she was so nice to me, because she is really pretty and all the guys walk into walls when she is around, but she isn't rude like you would expect her to be. We got stuck taking care of the babies in the nursery one time, and since it was just the two of us surrounded by screaming runny nosed toddlers, we did like a tag-team kind of babysitting service. She would get the kids to stop crying by rocking them, and I would distract them by pretending I was a tiger crawling over to eat them. Of course, some of the kids were apparently afraid of tigers, because not all of them liked my rendition of Little Sambo.

Anyhoo, Tiffany and I got to be friends, and it was really funny to see her fifth grade picture smiling up at me out of the yearbook.

Kids were starting to come into the library, so I closed the book and put the annuals back on the shelf. As I was walking out the door, Miss Sellwood, the librarian, asked if I had found what I was looking for. I was going to say yes, but then it occurred to me that she actually might be able to help me somehow. I asked her if there were any recent stories in the paper about a kid being kidnapped or missing. Her smile kind of faded; I think she was a bit shocked by my question. She told me where I could look up all the articles in the paper from past weeks on the computer. I thanked her, and felt her eyes on my back as I walked out of the library.

It was hard to concentrate at school, what with all the excitement in my head. Since Ashley was back from her Grandma's, I passed a note to her in class that said, "Meet me in the library at lunchtime."

Our class has developed quite a sophisticated system for passing notes. When a kid had a note that they wanted to pass, they would raise both hands up in the air while yawning. This alerted the whole class that a note would soon be in motion, without making Ms. Krump think they had a question or needed the bathroom pass. Then, the yawning kid would open a book while at the same time dropping the note on the floor next to a kid on the side of the room where the note was going. From that point, kids would see the name on the front of the note and slide the folded paper in the right direction until it got to the right person. So far, no one had ever been caught, and nobody tattled, because that would erase any chance they might have of ever getting a note.

Anyhoo, after the note went through the grapevine, Ashley

read it and then looked over and nodded to me. Ashley and Delight and I usually hang out together at recess and lunch. I like them because they are both really funny and really smart. We also have a friend named John, but he isn't in Ms. Krump's class, so we only see him after school. There are a lot of kids at our school so we have different recess times for the different classes, and the only time we really see him during school is at assemblies. John is an artist, and he is really smart. A lot of times while people are jabbering away trying to figure something out, he will just sit there and doodle, and you don't even know he was paying attention until out of the blue he figures out the answer to whatever we were trying to figure out.

The four of us met in second grade when we were all in the same class. I think Ashley used to have a bit of a crush on John because he is really cute, but she still won't admit it to this day. Since she is sort of a tomboy even though she likes to wear make-up, I don't think she wants anyone to know she has a soft side. I knew it all along though, because her favorite color is purple. How can you stay mad at a person in a purple shirt?

Anyhoo, it seemed like the morning took twelve hours to go by, but the lunch bell finally rang, and I grabbed my lunch and took off toward the library. Delight was in the special class helping the wheelchair kids (she likes to help them pop wheelies when no one is looking) and Ashley is a really good artist so she has an art class she gets to go to right before lunch. I'm kind of a math whiz so I take an extra math class before lunch. Our school is really great that way—at the beginning of the year we get to choose from about 15 different subjects and we get to spend a half hour every Friday in that class if we don't get into trouble during the week.

Since I got to the library before anyone else, I went back to the yearbook section and started up where I left off this morning. I heard Ashley and Delight talking as they entered the library, and looked up to greet them.

"What are you doing?" they asked simultaneously.

I was anticipating this question, of course, since I hadn't had time to tell either of them my new discovery about the boy. In fact, Ashley didn't know ANYTHING about ANY of it. Since we were in the library, I had to whisper, but I gave them both a run-down of my thoughts. Since I had been the only one to see the kid, my friends couldn't help look for his picture, but they said they would go into the computer program and try to find anything about a missing kid.

I went back to my books, and at the very end of last year's annual I saw a picture of Jer. We call him Jer even though his name is Jeramiah. Part of the reason we call him Jer is that everyone always spells his name wrong. They try to put an E where the A goes (Jeremiah) but just about any doofus can spell "J-E-R" right.

Jer lives two houses down from me. He moved here from a logging town, and even though he is only sixteen he has a really AWESOME truck. He is always outside working on it, and it makes a loud rumbly sound when he starts it up. He wears big boots and it seems like he is about ten feet tall. I call him Paul Bunyan and he calls me Babe, which is the name of Paul Bunyan's blue ox. Sometimes Jer lets me go for rides with him in his truck and he will drive out in really deep mud that goes flying up around the windows and splats on the trees as we fly by them. He's great.

Jer has a sister named Bethany that is a year older than me, and I think she seems really cool, but every time I see her she is on her cell phone, so we have never really had much of a chance to talk. I guess I could get her number from Jer and give her a call.

So anyhoo, here was a picture of Jer in sixth grade. That must have been right after he moved here. As I looked closer at the picture, I noticed that he was one of those people who didn't look much different even though he was a couple of years older. The only real difference was that it was the first time I'd seen him outside his truck.

I was just about to start on the next book, when Ashley yelled, "Hey Charlie, come here!"

She had apparently found something good enough to make her forget that Miss Sellwood gets VERY cranky when people are noisy in the library. I'm not sure why that is, since the only people who come in here are kids, and kids don't care if other kids are making noise in the library. I guess it's just one of those mysteries I may never understand.

I went over to the computer, and stopped short when I saw the picture on the screen. In fact, I just about stopped breathing. It was him. Ashley had found a picture of the kid in the gray car.

Chapter Six

I couldn't believe it.

"Print it out," said Delight. We all scrounged around for some money and came up with 17 cents between the three of us. The library charges five cents a copy to print something out, so I was hoping the newspaper piece was not more than 3 pages.

It turned out to be a short article, so we printed out three copies so we would each have the kid's picture. It had been written almost seven weeks ago, so enough time had gone by for the kid to have needed to get a haircut.

We took our copies and left the library so Miss Sellwood would stop glaring at us.

According to the article, the kid's name was Chris Thomas. He had been eight at the time of the abduction, and no one had

any information about it. So I had been right! It's weird how I
had just had a feeling that he was kidnapped or something. I
read on to find out that he had ridden his bike to the park after
school, and that was the last time anyone saw him. A reward
was offered for anyone giving information to the police that
led to his recovery. The article finished up by saying he had last
been seen wearing a white sweatshirt, blue jeans, black tennis
shoes, and a red coat with a picture of a bull on it. Well that sure
wasn't the way he was dressed when I saw him, but it was the
same kid, judging from the picture. Even though he had a wide,
happy grin in the photograph, I could tell it was the same face.

Just then, the warning bell rang, which meant we only had
five minutes to eat lunch and get back to class. We were too
busy wolfing down our food to talk much, but I managed to tell
the others through mouthfuls that this was the kid. My mom
would really have hated having to spend my lunchtime with
me. She thinks it is really gross if food accidentally falls out of
your mouth while you are talking. I don't know what the big
deal is. It's not like I'm going to pick it up and eat it again.
Sometimes food just flies out if you use words that have certain
consonants in them and you have food in your mouth. Like the
letter P. Or words with TH in them. Or SH. One time I was
talking to my dad during dinner and Dallin tucked his ear in
(I'm not sure how he does this, but somehow he takes the

pointed part of his ears and pushes it into the hole, and they just stay there) and I thought it looked funny so I started laughing, and said, "Dallin, STOP it!" Well, when I said the word STOP, a bunch of food came flying out of my mouth and stuck right onto my dad's glasses. You can only imagine how much trouble that got me into. But I was careful not to spray my friends in my excitement about Chris.

It was hard to concentrate for the rest of the day, but the bell finally sounded and we poured out of school. Have you ever heard that there is a furry little animal called a lemming and sometimes a bunch of them will just run together in a herd right off a cliff or into the water? Watching the kids pour out of my school at the end of the day always reminds me of a bunch of lemmings running down the steps.

Anyhoo, The four of us always meet at the big fir tree in front of the school so we can walk together. John was already there, and when I saw him I remembered that he still didn't know anything about Chris. I pulled out the newspaper article while I walked over to him, and told him about what I had seen. John, ever the practical one, said, "Cool! How much money do you think the reward will be?"

I hadn't actually thought about a reward, but if I got a crisp 50 dollar bill out of it that would rock.

As we walked, the conversation drifted to other topics.

There is a corner where we usually split up and go our separate ways, and we have a hand-slap thing where the four of us do a high five in the air and clap hands before we split up. As I was tossing my hand in the air to say goodbye, I saw a long gray car driving around the corner. Since I was just standing there, my friends followed my gaze. Before I even thought about what I was doing, I yelled, "C'mon!" and ran after the car. That wasn't as futile as it sounds; the speed limit in our neighborhood is 25 mph, and we know LOTS of shortcuts. So it really isn't a big deal to outrun a car if you know the area. The trick is in anticipating where it will turn, since you have to stay ahead of it.

I couldn't see inside the car from that distance, but it had looked like there were two people in the back seat and one in front. I was guessing the one in front was probably the same driver I had seen the first time. I wondered if the kidnapper was in the back with Chris, or if they had only let him ride in the car that one time and then tossed him back down into the dungeon when they got home. I had visions of his plate made of bent up metal with a piece of bread on it and a dingy metal cup with cloudy water in it for him to drink. The more I thought about it, the sorrier for him I felt, as I dodged in and out of the yards of my neighbors. Every now and then as I climbed over a fence or squeezed through some bushes, I would catch a glimpse of the back of the car as it turned a corner, or I would see the front of it turn the opposite direction I had been expecting, and I would have to double back and catch up to them.

My friends were right behind me, as we had done this a few times before, and all four of us were in pretty good shape. I'm telling you, riding a bike every day gives you some great muscles for running! I had anticipated that the car would turn onto Main street, but it slowed to a stop before it got there. It pulled into a driveway about halfway down the street and then the garage door went up. We all jumped behind the wall of the house we had been in front of, and peeked around to see who got out. Unfortunately, the car pulled into the garage and the door shut behind it. They must have gone in the house through a door inside the garage, because that was the last we saw of them.

But at least we had a tentative address. I didn't have the heart to tell my friends I hadn't been able to get close enough to see if the license number was the same as the one we were looking for, but the car looked the same to me, so I was hopeful.

We decided to walk out onto the sidewalk and nonchalantly glance at the address of the house and find a way to get a look at the people inside. The address was 831 Adams Street. As we neared the place, Delight said, "Hey! I've got a great idea!"

She took off her backpack and started rummaging through

it. "Since we just came from school, I still have my choir candy bars to sell," she said. "Maybe we can go up and ring the doorbell and ask if they want to buy any."

GREAT idea. We walked up the steps and when we got to the landing at the top, we just kind of looked at each other. Somehow it had seemed like a better idea when we were further away from the house. I'm sure each of us had our own morbid fantasy of how the kidnappers would grab us and throw us downstairs with their other prisoner.

Finally, since this whole thing was my doing, I rang the doorbell. We waited. We looked at each other. We waited. After what seemed like an hour, John rang the doorbell again.

"Maybe they are pretending not to be home and that's why they won't answer the door," said Ashley.

I was starting to hope she was right, when we heard footsteps coming toward us from the inside of the house. It was too late to turn back now.

Chapter Seven

I don't know why we were so scared; the people in the house didn't know we knew anything, and anyway, I wasn't even sure if it was the right car. As the door creaked open (yes, it even sounded like a scary movie) we looked into the eyes of a very old, broken down looking lady who was shorter than we were. Not knowing what we were supposed to do then, we all just stood there stupidly. After a moment, the lady coaxed us, obviously seeing the candy in Ashley's hand.

"Are you selling candy to raise money?" she asked kindly.

"Y-yes," Ashley sputtered.

The lady waited for her to say more, but Ashley looked as if her lips were suddenly made of cement and they refused to open. Finally, the woman asked how much they were. Ashley told her they were a dollar, and the lady disappeared inside the house, presumably to go get her purse, and more probably to pick up a hatchet on the way to chop us to bits. As soon as she was out of sight, all four of us started talking at once. Mostly, I admit, everyone was talking at ME, asking if I was sure it was the right car, and wanting to know if the license plate had been the right number. I told them that the car I had seen the other day had the license plate KNH831, but that the car had been too far away for me to see the plate on the car in this garage. Right about then, the lady came back, and gave us three dollars and Ashley gave her three chocolate bars. We thanked her, and as we turned to go, John's face turned white. I looked in the same direction he was facing, to see what he was reacting to. Then, I saw it, and I knew why he looked the way he did. I hadn't made the connection before, and it was only because we had been talking about the license plate that I made it now. Ashley and Delight noticed our expressions, but knew enough to not say anything until we were a few houses away.

Finally, Delight couldn't stand it any longer, and said, "WHAT???"

Without saying a word, John and I both pointed at the house we had just come from. If there had been any doubt when we saw that sweet old lady, it was erased now. Delight and Ashley stared in the direction of our fingers, still not comprehending what it meant. Then, softly, Ashley's face registered understanding. She looked at Delight and said, "The number on the house is 831. That's the same number as the one on the license plate of the car."

Chapter Eight

The coincidence seemed too uncanny. There had to be a connection. As we walked home in silence, each of us deep in thought, I wondered just what kind of connections a person would need to create such an elaborate scheme. I wondered if they had special ordered the license plate to match the house, kind of like Jer, who has a license plate he had made up that says "CHOMP." I asked him about it once and he said his truck eats other trucks for lunch, so that's why he had the plate made. Anyhoo, I suppose the kidnappers could have driven around looking for a house that was for sale with the right number too. It seemed like a lot more trouble to do it that way though. But either way, why would they want their car to give away their location like that? We all pondered the questions that piled up, unanswered, as we walked home.

As we came upon the corner once more to split up, our high five was half-hearted and perfunctory, like a kiss you give your mother when you are on the phone and preoccupied with your conversation.

As I walked up the steps to my house, I decided to show my family the newspaper clipping and see what they thought about it. I wanted to tell them about how the house had the same license plate number, but my parents had a tendency to think my imagination was running off with me, and I still didn't REALLY know anything yet.

At dinner, I asked my parents if they remembered reading in the paper about a kid in the neighborhood who had been kidnapped.

"Why yes," said my mother as she passed the corn, "Wasn't that just a few months ago?"

"I think so," I replied cautiously. I didn't want them to know I had researched this and make them wonder what I was up to. I showed them the article from the paper and told them I had seen it when I was in the library at school and wondered if he lived in our neighborhood. Well, that WAS true.

"I know that kid," piped up Dallin, "He used to walk to school with Jon The Alien."

Now, ordinarily, I would ignore such a statement, but I

wanted to check out every possible lead, so I had no choice but to ask what the haybells Dallin was talking about.

"Oh, Jon told me he is an alien from the planet Pluto," Dallin explained. "He says he is green with antennae coming out of his head, and he just turned 327 years old."

I couldn't resist.

"Why did he have to TELL you he was green? Couldn't you just see it when you look at him?" I asked.

Dallin rolled his eyes, and with exaggerated patience, informed me that any idiot knows aliens can change into human form to keep us from discovering their true nature. I felt my face grow red with irritation, but I didn't want to get into an argument with him and have my parents intervene and NEVER know how this alien person was involved with Chris Thomas. So I changed the subject.

"Wow, that's cool," I said casually. "So how did he know the missing kid?"

Dallin wasn't used to positive attention from me, so he milked it for all it was worth. "Well," he boasted, "At recess I saw the two of them over by the fence. The kid from the paper was pointing at the hospital across the street and they got in an argument. I was thinking that there was gonna be a fight, so I kept watching them. Jon is a couple of years younger, so I knew he was gonna get pounded."

Everyone sat expectantly waiting for more information, but my brother just sat there, glowing from the attention. After a moment, when it sank in that we were listening for further details, he faltered a little, as there seemingly weren't any more. Since he still had the floor, he dove into a detailed description of what kind a of planet Pluto is. I really couldn't care less, so I tuned out and concentrated on my own thoughts.

So Chris DID go to my school. At least he was on school grounds, which made me wonder how many other people may have seen him there. I made a mental list of the facts:

Chris Thomas was the name of the kid in the gray car.

The article said he was 8 years old at the time he disappeared, which was a couple of months ago.

There was something about the hospital that bothered him enough to get into an argument about it.

Hey! That's it! I could go to the hospital and ask if anyone from his family worked there or had been a patient. I excused myself from the table, and told my parents I was going to go for a bike ride. Mom opened her mouth, but before she could speak, I said, "Yes, my homework is all done." So she smiled and said okay.

The hospital was across the street from the elementary school, which was only about six blocks from my house. I rode like the wind, thinking the whole time about what I was going to say. Since I didn't know the family at all, I would just have to go in and ask to see Chris Thomas' parents. That way I would know if someone had been a patient there or if they worked at the hospital. Hopefully it wouldn't sound too suspicious.

As I got to the parking lot of the hospital, I scanned for the gray car. I found myself doing that automatically these days, no matter where I was. Not seeing it, I parked and locked my bike, and went inside.

I used to always plug my nose whenever I went into a hospital. There is a weird smell in there that reminds me of science lab at school. John told me it is the smell of dead, rotting bodies that they pile up in the basement, but I think that is illegal. Since I was trying to be grown up, I didn't plug my nose, but I sure didn't breathe in through it either.

I walked around until I saw a lady sitting at a desk. She was wearing a smock-type thing with a sweater over it, and she had a stethoscope so I figured she could probably help me. As I walked toward her, the phone at her desk rang, and she smiled at me as she answered it.

Don't you think it's kind of funny that you just KNOW what someone is thinking sometimes in that type of situation? Like I could almost hear her saying, "I'll help you in just a second, but I have to answer the phone first." But if she had ignored me, I wouldn't have thought she wanted to help me and I might have tried to find someone else to ask, but I just stood there waiting for her to get off the phone since I knew that was what she wanted me to do. I think that is pretty weird.

Anyhoo, after a minute she got off the phone, and said, "Sorry to make you wait. Can I help you?"

Silently pleased with myself for knowing she would say just that, I said, "I am looking for Chris Thomas' parents. Could you help me find them, or maybe page them for me?"

The lady stopped smiling and her face went dead serious. I was starting to wonder if I had made a dangerous mistake by coming here, when she said, "I'm Chris' mother. Do you know where he is?"

Chapter Nine

Maybe I'm just paranoid, but I couldn't be sure that this lady REALLY was Chris' mom. She could have been some imposter planted there to fool people like me. After all, it was pretty elaborate planning on someone's part to have matching house and license plate numbers. I wasn't sure just how far they would go. I decided to play it safe.

"I have a friend that goes to the same school as Chris and he said you worked here," I offered lamely.

She looked disappointed, but said, "Yes, I work here. You do know that Chris has been missing for 2 months don't you?"

The poor woman looked so torn up I decided she probably really was his mom, and I really wanted to tell her what I had seen. Also, being a grown-up, she might have better luck involving the police than I would, since I was just a kid. One time I called the police to tell them I had cut myself. I was only about five years old, and my mom was in the shower so I didn't want to bother her. The 911 operator had been pretty rude when I was trying to explain how I had fallen down the steps and gashed open my leg. All she cared about was whether or not I had an adult in the house. I said no, because at the time I didn't know what that word meant, and I thought she was asking me if I had a DOLT in the house-like a dorky person. They traced the call somehow and came to the house, and when they asked where my parents were, I took them to my mom. She wasn't expecting company in the bathroom, so I got in a lot of trouble for that one.

Anyhoo, I told Mrs. Thomas everything I knew, and she seemed pretty excited about the fact that he was still alive. I guess it WOULD be pretty gruesome to just have a person in your family disappear and not know if they were dead or alive. She told me Chris had a sister that goes to my school named Sarah. I decided to try to get to know her a little bit. Mrs. Thomas said it was almost time for her break and offered to fill me in on some details if I had time, so I stayed around for a while and talked to her.

The scoop is that Chris was on his way home from school. His mom always told him to walk with someone, but I guess he didn't listen, since he was alone when he left the school. That's it. They pretty much didn't know anything else, except what he was wearing when he left in the morning. The really creepy part is that I used to always walk home alone before I became friends with Delight and Ashley and John. Just think, that could have been me. Well, maybe. It was weird to think about.

Anyhoo, Mrs. Thomas went back to work, and I left the hospital and rode home. Alone. I kept a wary eye out for strange cars trying to lure me into their clutches. I don't want to make you scared or anything, but it's not easy being a kid anymore. You have to watch out for stuff like that. I made it home okay, and went straight up to my room and called Ashley.

Ashley had been in a class with a girl named Sarah, and I didn't know if it was Chris' sister, but I wanted to find out. Ashley said she couldn't remember. She put the phone down so she could get the school annual and see what her last name was. "BINGO!" Ashley yelled excitedly into the phone. "Sarah Thomas! That's her!"

I wasn't sure what Sarah could tell us that her mom hadn't already said, but I wanted to find out if she knew the kids he'd hung out with at school. Other than the Plutonian Alien.

Chapter Ten

I had been planning to go to the library and look through the annuals to find Sarah's picture, but I lucked out—on the way there, I heard Darric (THE dreamiest guy in the world) yell, "Hey Sarah!" in the hallway. I turned around, and the girl he was talking to looked so much like the kid in the paper I knew it had to be her. As usual, Darric was with Kyle, a kid that was so tall he almost had to duck to get through doorways. He looked kinda scary but fortunately he was a gentle type of giant.

I didn't waste time; I walked right up to her and asked if she was Sarah Thomas. At first she just looked at me kinda funny, but then she said, "Yes, and you are…." I told her I thought I might have some information about her little brother. I expected her to have the same kind of reaction her mom had, but she just stared blankly at me like she didn't even HAVE a brother. Even though I knew she was the right girl, I was confused enough by her reaction that I said, "You know, Chris? I think I saw him."

Then, she grabbed my arm and dragged me over to her notebook and shouted "WHERE DID YOU SEE HIM?" while at the same time looking for something to write with. I recited the story about how I'd seen him in the car, and how I followed the car to the house, and then she stopped me by grabbing my arm and looking so intently into my face I wasn't sure if she was going to give me a headbutt.

"Where was the house?" She demanded.

I told her, and realized foolishly that I had been so intent on remembering the house number, I could no longer remember the street name. I thought it was something that started with an A, and it was a person's name. Andrews Street? Amanda Street? Albert Street? I just couldn't remember.

The school bell rang, so I promised her I would meet her after school and went to my first class. ADAMS STREET! That's what it was. I grabbed a pen out of my notebook and wrote it on my hand so I wouldn't forget it again.

After school, Sarah and Kyle and Darric were waiting for me by the big fir tree. I guess Darric was with her because they were kind of in the process of hooking up. Kyle and John talked about sports-type stuff while we waited for Delight and

Ashley to get there. Then, we all regurgitated our pieces of the story, and when I told about what Dallin had seen, Sarah interrupted me.

"That must have been the day before he disappeared! He was upset when he got home, because some kid at school had said he was from a different planet and he was going to suck up the hospital and send it to Pluto!"

Sounds like something Jon would say.

Suddenly, I got an idea. I knew my brother Wade was coming over tonight to pick up the CD I had borrowed from him. I had made a copy of this really weird song called, "OLD MUSTARD" that is about a kid who had a sandwich in his room even though he wasn't supposed to eat in there, and when his mom opened the door unexpectedly he threw it under the mattress and then he forgot all about it for about 3 months until it took on a life of its own and formed it's own singing group consisting of moldy condiments.

Anyhoo, I could ask him to drive me over to the house on Adams Street and see if I could find out anything new.

Delight had to help with an emergency when she got home, so she couldn't go with me. It seems that baby Dannielle came upstairs licking her hands and arms and was all sticky—even spots in her hair. Upon investigation, they found that Amanda had been playing in the food storage room. In the 5 gallon bucket of brown sugar to be precise. I could hear Delight's mom in the background yelling for someone to come help her. As Delight was hanging up the phone, I could hear a swift spanking, and a tiny voice saying, "Baby Dannielle opened the bucket." Yeah right.

John had homework to do, and Ashley was taking Jennifer to the library for a home school project, so I decided to just go by myself. As I neared my house, I saw Wade's car out front. He and Jer were out in the driveway talking about cars. I could tell what they were talking about before I was even close enough to hear them, because of the way their faces were so animated.

"I'll give you a quarter if you give me a ride!" I called out to Wade.

"Sorry kid, I'm waiting for Jer to help me tune this clunker of mine," he called back to me. He always called his cars clunkers, even though they were in perfect condition. Jer liked to come over and look under the hood and just stand there saying, "WOW." That's guy talk for, "I want your car." Guys are funny.

Oh well. I could just ride my bike over again. The sky looked a bit cloudy but it probably wouldn't rain, so I could make a quick trip of it. I ran into the house and stuck a note on the fridge saying I'd be home by dinnertime, and grabbed my bike out of the garage. After a mile or so, the clouds started getting darker, and before I knew it, rain started POURING down on me. A meteorologist I am not.

Chapter Eleven

Since I was almost to Adams Street, I didn't let the rain slow me down. I slowed to a stop in front of the house and noticed that a light was on downstairs. Why do you suppose prisoners are always kept in the dungeon? Maybe because you can't see them walking around if you peek in the windows. I rode around the block to see if there was a way to get to the back yard. The rain was REALLY coming down now, which was good because no one was outside to see me. Rain also makes it harder to see someone sneaking around in the bushes since the rain is also moving them around.

I parked my bike behind a big green bush and tiptoed over to the window with the light on. It was dirty, but I wasn't sure if it was smart to wipe it off with my hand, because that might leave my fingerprints around the place. I opted to wipe it with the arm of my jacket, and peered inside.

I couldn't see too much, but it looked like there was a table, a chair, a couple of old mattresses, a washing machine, and a box with clothes in it. Well, that certainly looked incriminating! The only thing that would have made it look MORE like a kidnapping scene would be to have a kid tied in the chair.

I strained to see Chris somewhere, but the room was empty. Satisfied that there wasn't anything else to see, I got up. As I turned to get my bike, a hand gripped my shoulder.

I was dead meat.

Chapter Twelve

I had a fleeting hope that it was somehow the sweet little old lady grabbing my shoulder. Guess again. It was a burly guy with arms the size of a Buick. I didn't know how much he had seen, or how long he had been watching me, so I had to think fast.

It's funny what happens to you when a huge scary man is grabbing your shoulder. I know that people say their life flashes before their eyes when they think they are going to die, but all I could think about was how I was going to get my bike home. Before he had a chance to ask what I was doing looking in his window, I got an idea. Grown-ups usually don't expect kids to be smart, so I formulated a plan to trick him.

"Oh, hi!" I said brightly, pretending he hadn't startled me at all. "I noticed your windows are pretty dirty. You probably don't have time to clean them, and I will do it for 25 cents a window. Would you like me to clean them for you?"

He stood there, baffled. Perfect. Then, he stuttered, "N-no…I don't care if my windows are dirty." After a minute, his eyes narrowed and he asked where my squeegee and water bucket were. I had to think fast.

"Oh, I'm just going around the neighborhood drumming up business today," I said. "Tomorrow is the day I do the actual cleaning." He seemed content with that, and told me to get lost. WHEW! I grabbed my bike and rode over to the house next door, and peered into the window of the basement to make it look more convincing. Thank goodness no one was home.

When I looked over my shoulder, the scary dude was gone, and I relaxed a little. Man, I'd almost had to change my shorts over that one. I was gonna have to be more careful. HE sure looked closer to what I had expected than the sweet little old lady had. And the basement was the perfect set-up for a prisoner. There was even a place to sleep with those mattresses piled on the floor. I decided I had enough proof to take it to the police.

When I got home, I took the phone into my room and shut the door. I didn't want anyone to overhear me talking to the cops, because my family had a tendency to over react when I got involved in mysteries. I guess they were afraid some big burly guy might grab me or something. Sissies.

Well, it's a good thing I didn't have an emergency, because when I called 911 they actually put me on hold! Can you believe it? When they finally got on the phone, I asked if they could give me the number to the regular police station because I couldn't find the phone book. The lady was really mean about it and told me that people like ME calling were the reason emergencies had to be put on hold. Since she had a valid point, I didn't say anything obnoxious, I just waited patiently for her to give me the phone number. Then, I called the police station and got put on hold again for about 20 minutes. The guy I finally DID talk to kept saying, "Uh huh, uh huh," like he was reading a book while he was talking to me.

After telling the officer everything I knew, I asked if I should fill out some papers or something, and he said, "No, we'll take it from here. You just make sure to keep yourself safe by staying away from the house. We don't want TWO missing kids."

Oh MAN.

I was really messed up now, because I didn't want to go against the order of a policeman, but I didn't just want to give up on the case either. I would have to find a way to do both.

I could smell brownies cooking downstairs, so I headed

down for a snack. I like to spread peanut butter on them and sprinkle them with sesame seeds. It sounds kind of weird, but it is really tasty. I learned about it by accident one time when I put peanut butter on a brownie and then knocked over the sesame seeds when I was putting the peanut butter away. The top was open, so they dumped all over the place. I decided to try a bite of it before I scraped off the peanut butter. Hey, what can I say? I'm adventurous.

The brownies my dad made were still hot, so the peanut butter melted when I put it on. YUM! While I was eating I got to thinking about Chris, and how he was probably eating moldy scraps of bread for dinner. I resolved to find out what I could do to help. Since tomorrow was Saturday, I knew I would have a whole day to work on the mystery. I didn't know if I should have my friends help, or go it alone, since it might be dangerous.

I went up to my room and got my pajamas on. Then I climbed into bed and turned off the light so I could look at the stars. It helps to look at stars when you want to think clearly, for some reason. I reviewed the information I had collected so far:

Chris Thomas had been kidnapped about 2 months ago.

His sister, Sarah, goes to my school, and his mom works at the hospital.

Chris was in the back seat of a gray car AFTER he had been kidnapped.

I saw a car go into a garage with the same number on the house as the number on the license plate.

WAIT a minute. I never did actually confirm that the same car that went into the garage was the one that I had seen the kid in. The coincidence had been so uncanny I had just ASSUMED it was the same car. I had to do a stake-out to find out for sure. I would sit someplace where I could see the car come out of the garage, and then get a look at the license plate. Since I had already been seen near the house, I didn't want to take a chance of getting caught again. I would need to sit quite a distance away, and just bring my binoculars.

Don't know how I ever got by without my binoculars. Initially, I had bought them to spy on my new neighbors, since when they moved in it had been about three in the morning. They never came out of the house and I figured they were drug dealers or something, so naturally I had gone out and bought binoculars to watch them. It turned out that they moved in and then went on vacation, so they weren't even home. Then, as you know, Ashley ended up being one of my best friends.

Anyhoo, I set my alarm for six in the morning so I could get over to the kidnapper's house before anyone left. Most people sleep in on Saturday, so I was hoping to get over there before anyone woke up.

Chapter Thirteen

When I had gone to bed it had seemed like a great idea to get up at six in the morning. But when my alarm went off, I just rolled over in bed and turned it off. I was too sleepy to get up. I tried to go back to sleep, but kind of just laid there for a while thinking. I had been dreaming about going over to the house, and in my dream the guy that grabbed me had been driving a car, and he ran over me and started laughing that wild "bad-guy" laugh that you always hear in cartoons and movies. It kind of scared me. I wondered if I really SHOULD just let the police handle it. But I kind of felt an obligation to the kid, since he had looked me in the eye and asked me for help with his expression. I didn't just want to give upon him.

I stumbled out of bed and went downstairs to eat breakfast. Even though the memory of the dream was still fresh in my mind, I had to find a way to help Chris. By the time I was done eating, I had decided to go over to Adams street and do whatever I could to rescue him, but I'd do everything possible to keep myself safe.

I got dressed and left a note on the table that said I was going to go bike riding, so no one would expect me to be home for a long time. It seemed to only take me a second to get to the house, since I was lost in thought while I rode. It's funny how time is kind of rubbery like that. You know, like how waiting for school to get out takes forever, but that SAME 15 minutes goes by lightening fast when you are at the park with your friends. I wonder why that is?

Anyhoo, I got out my binoculars and sat down under a big fir tree across the street. It was a perfect location, because the tree had great big branches that obscured me, but I could easily see the house. At first I just sat there, but then I wondered if I could see in the windows with the binoculars. I focused them and looked around. The drapes were open a little bit, and I could see what looked like a couch and table, and what looked like a kitchen entrance, but not much else. Since I had cleaned the basement window with my sleeve, I looked over there to see if the kid was downstairs. Rats. I was too high up to see in the basement.

After about a half hour, I got bored, so I started looking

around the neighborhood with the binoculars. It looked like the people in the house next door were having a fight, because they were standing really close together and the man was shaking his finger at the woman. I just love trying to figure out what is going on by looking at how people are standing or by their facial expressions.

I was so busy watching the other stuff going on, I almost missed the gray car pulling out of the driveway. As I swept the binoculars back across the street, I caught the car in my lens as it was leaving. I quickly looked down to check the plate. WRS 248. Boy did THAT put me in a rotten mood.

I got on my bike and slowly just rode around for a while. Rats. I didn't know where the kidnappers were keeping him after all. Or, was it possible that they had CHANGED the license plate after the day that I had seen it? That seemed like a lot of trouble to go to. But maybe not. The car really did look like the one I had seen that first day. My brain was starting to hurt.

I decided to treat myself to a twistee cone to help me think more clearly. There is a place here in town that will toss candy sprinkles on your ice cream cone for only 10 cents extra. After all this stress I needed a sugar fix.

When I got to the diner to get my ice cream, I went through the drive thru on my bike. It's kind of fun to do that just to see the look on the workers' faces. While I was ordering, I couldn't believe it—the gray car pulled up behind me!! I was so stunned, I forgot to order. I just kind of stood there and stuttered. When I got my wits about me enough to order, I pedaled forward and surreptitiously looked behind me to check out the license plate. IT WAS THE RIGHT CAR. I started to think a million miles a minute. I was going to have to follow them somehow, but on my bike that would be hard.

I got my cone and rode my bike around the corner so they couldn't see me. Because of the way the street was, they would have to turn left when they got out of the drive thru, so I started riding on the street and hoped to get enough of a head start that it wouldn't look like I was following them. Sure enough, a few minutes later, they passed me. Fortunately, there was a lot of traffic, and the lights were red enough of the time for me to follow them without too much trouble. We were headed in the direction of Adams Street, so I started wondering if they had 2 cars that looked alike that they parked at the same house or something. Just then, they turned the corner at Oak Street. I knew it was a dead end, so I slowed to a stop as I got to the corner, and just stood there watching which house they would go to. I was amazed when they just parked on the street. Maybe they were only there to visit.

Even though they were a couple of blocks from me, I got a

good look at the guy driving. He had a chauffer uniform on, but he had long, stringy blonde hair sticking out of the back of his hat. He went around and opened the door to the back, and a tall red haired woman got out. A WOMAN? After the encounter with the man with the iron grip, I'd decided that the kidnappers were probably huge burly men with long greasy hair and beady eyes. Maybe she was the housekeeper.

The lady went straight to the front door of the house and opened it, so whoever she was, she apparently lived there. I couldn't see the address of the house, so I moved in closer. It seemed unlikely they would come back out right away, so I felt pretty safe. WRONG!!! As soon as I was 50 feet from the place they came back outside and went to the trunk of the car. I tried not to appear nervous, and when I saw that the trunk was full of groceries, I got an idea.

"Can I help you carry your groceries in?" I asked as casually as possible, trying not to let on that my knees were knocking bruises into each other.

"No." She said. Just like that. Not, "no thank you", just no. Maybe she WAS a bad guy. I REALLY wasn't sure what else to do, so I just kind of stood there watching them, and when she had a large bag in each arm, I got off my bike and said, "Let me get the door for you."

I didn't know if she would just drop the groceries and punch me, but I had to try something. To my utter amazement, she smiled and said that would be nice. I leaped up the small stairway and opened the screen door for her. As she walked in, I gazed around the room. It was pretty empty except for a TV and some old ugly couches. Maybe the reason they had kidnapped Chris was for the ransom money.

She made several more trips to the car, and I just stood there holding the screen door open. I heard the chauffer call her "Polly" and when I thought about it later, it seemed odd to me that she was carrying in the groceries at all, since that should have been his job. Maybe he just wanted to LOOK like a chauffer, but he really wasn't one.

I heard the sound of the trunk closing, and as she came up the walk, Polly said thank you for my help and I smiled at her and let the door bang shut. Before I left, I made sure to look up at the address on the house. I looked around but couldn't see one. I guess they took it down when they decided to hide out there. I knew the house number would be easy enough to figure out by looking at the numbers on the houses on either side, so I went next door. That number was 437. The number on the house on the left side was 417, so I guessed their house number was 427.

I was pretty excited as I rode my bike home. Now that I had some relatively solid evidence, should I go to the police? It seemed like the obvious thing to do. At first I wanted to ride there, but decide that it would probably be better just to call on the phone and see how they reacted

When I got home, I heard the screaming before I even got inside. My brother Dallin was in the kitchen with a knife in one hand and a red puddle in the other. My mom was trying to calm him down, but he wasn't paying her much attention. There was a block of cheese on the counter so I could pretty much put two and two together and figure out what happened. We finally got him all bandaged up and cleaned up the mess, but I gave up the idea of telling my mom the news about finding the kidnappers. She wasn't too good with surprises, and my brother took up the quota for the day. So, I just snuck the phone up to my room to call the police.

I called a bunch of different numbers, and left detailed messages at them all, because I wasn't sure which department at the police station took care of kidnappers. I didn't want to call 911 because it really wasn't an emergency. So, after leaving messages with the Detectives, the Human Resources Department, Information, and the District Attorney's office, I figured I was covered. Initially, I wasn't going to leave my name or number, but then I remembered that there might be a reward. Hey, I'm not stupid. So I left my name and information, and then I went to bed. And waited.

Chapter Fourteen

I took my time getting ready for school the next day, hoping to get a call before I left, but the phone didn't ring. I didn't want them to call and talk to my mom, since I hadn't talked to her yet myself, but she was going to be gone all day at her "mural painting adventure," so I wasn't too worried. She had decided to paint a mural with a bunch of her friends, so they were spending a lot of time lately with spray paint cans out by the railroad. Unlike kids, they had asked permission from the owners to slather the wall with graffiti but instead of words they were making a picture. It kind of seems like asking for permission would take all the fun out of it, but I guess not, since she was spending a lot of time there lately.

Anyhoo, I went to school and told my friends about what had happened. During social studies, Darric smiled at me and

I wondered what the chances were that he would dump Tiffany to be with me. Color that number ZERO. Meanwhile, our teacher was explaining the importance of some culture we were supposed to be studying about. She was telling us how to pronounce her first name in Spanish, which was kind of weird since you tend to forget that teachers even HAVE a first name. Hers is Angela. Don't ask me what it is in Spanish, because frankly I hadn't been paying all that much attention. She was one of those teachers that you could tell really cared about us, and I half considered asking for her help about the missing kid, but decided against it. I didn't want to get any more people involved until I had a plan.

When I got home there was a message on the answering machine for me from Lieutenant Eric Miller. It said he wanted me to call and tell him exactly what I knew about Chris Thomas, since he was in charge of the case. I called the number, and a man with a really deep voice answered the phone. I was kind of glad to unload this burden from my shoulders and talk to an adult about it, because it was pretty serious. He asked me lots of questions about whether or not I knew the kid when he was at my school, and stuff like that. When I told him the address of the place where the car had parked, his response startled me.

He asked if I was aware that I given him Chris' home address.

Chapter Fifteen

Of all the things I expected, what I did NOT expect was for Chris to be hiding out in his own house. Were they trying to fool the insurance company into paying a false ransom? Why did the house look so empty? I had to examine the facts as I knew them so far:

Chris Thomas was listed as missing, and I had seen him in a gray car with the license plate KNH 831.

Lieutenant Miller had said that the house Polly had gone to was where Chris lived.

There had been an article in the paper saying Chris' parents didn't know where he was.

Chris' sister Sarah had had a weird reaction when I told her I had seen Chris. The question she had asked me was "WHERE did you see him."

Chris' mom seemed to really not know where her son was.

Was Chris' sister hiding him? IF that was the case though, he wouldn't have been riding around in a car. I guessed that Polly was in on it since she was in the gray car Chris had been in. There wasn't too much furniture, so maybe they had moved out. This was starting to get really complicated. I had to get inside that house somehow. Maybe I could make friends with Sarah Thomas and go to her house after school.

I called Delight and asked she could come over. She had to babysit her sister again, so she couldn't. Rats. I called Ashley and asked her to come with me, but she was doing her homework and didn't think she would be able to get done in time. Double rats. I called John but he wasn't home. MAN! I really didn't want to go over there by myself, but I wanted to solve this mystery. I took a chance and went to Jer's house to see if his little sister might be home. We really didn't know each other too well, but she seemed nice, and I didn't want to go over alone.

When I knocked on the door, Bethany was the one to open it. Before I could even say anything, the phone rang. She asked me to come in and bolted over to the phone, and I could tell by her tone that it was a boy she liked. Bethany was only a year older than I was, but she definitely had a jump on me in the romance department. She always had smiley faces painted onto her nails or glitter in her hair. To be quite honest, I was somewhat envious of her confidence to do such things, but I would never have admitted that out loud. While she tried to get off the phone, I decided better of telling her my secret, and waved goodbye as I slipped out the door. Then, I went back home and left a note for my mom telling her I went to Sarah's house. I jumped on my bike and rode over to Oak Street, reminding myself all the way there that Chris needed my help. Gulp.

In a way, I was glad that I'd found out this was Chris' house, because it gave me a good reason to be there, since he had gone to my school. I was just going to pretend I didn't know he had been missing, and wanted to come over to his house and hang out with him. Okay, he was 3 years older than me. Okay, he was a boy. Okay, I had never met the guy. But I had the advantage of knowing that grown-ups often overlook such obvious inconsistencies.

When I got there, the car wasn't in front of the house. I went up the steps and knocked on the door. After a few seconds I knocked again. No one answered, so I went up to the window and peered in. Not only was there very little furniture, but there were no pictures on the walls or plants or anything that makes a house look lived in. I went back over to the door and knocked again. This time, I turned the knob to see if it was locked. I knew it would be wrong to go into someone else's house, but I figured this was a matter of life and death, sort of, and if Chris was tied to a chair someplace inside, now would be a perfect time to go in and find him.

It was locked. Rats. I decided to go around the house and look in the windows and try the back door to see if it was unlocked. When I went behind the first bush to look in the window, I stepped on the tail of a sleeping cat and just about wet my pants when it sprang to life. Yikes! It's not like I wasn't already jumpy enough!

The drapes on the windows were ugly and torn up. It was easy to see inside, but there wasn't much to see. Why would someone without any decent possessions lock their doors? You'd think they would BEG burglars to come in and take stuff—maybe even leave something behind from the previous job. It's possible they were afraid someone like me would walk in the door even though they weren't home.

I hate it when my conclusions make me look bad.

Since the front door was locked, I walked around the house and tried the back door. Just like magic, the knob turned and I heard the click of the door as it slipped open. I had pretty much talked myself into believing it would be locked, so it took a minute for me to register that I now had the opportunity to do something REALLY illegal and go inside.

Television doesn't show the viewers how terrifying it is to contemplate going into a person's house when you're not supposed to. On TV the cops act like it is no big deal. I, on the other hand, realized in a hurry that these people could have a huge dog on the other side of the door that was regularly poked into a rage and fed a steady diet of unwanted intruders just like myself. The dog image made my mind up for me, and I slammed the door shut.

As I paused to catch my breath, I heard a very faint noise. It seemed to be coming from the basement, and it sounded like a cat in distress, but the sound was really muffled. I had visions of breaking open the basement window to rescue Chris only to find a cat playing with a ball of string and watching it lick itself while the police dragged me off to prison.

I had to take a chance.

Chapter Sixteen

Wanting to be as cautious (and legal) as possible, I knocked loudly on the door. When no one came to the door, I again opened it, this time yelling at the top of my lungs, "HELLO!"

Again, I heard the strained muffled sounds coming from the basement. I mentally made up a story as I walked into the house...I was coming over to visit Chris and Sarah, and when I saw that the door was unlocked and heard noise inside, I thought they had called out for me to come in. Visions went through my head of the kind of fiery fate awaiting those who lied once they got to death's door, but I brushed them aside with the justification that Chris needed my help.

The house didn't have any lights on, and it was starting to get dark outside, making it difficult to see. I didn't want to alert anyone unnecessarily to the fact that I was there, so I just left the lights off and peered into the dark hallway. It was eerie how the whole house was void of furniture except for a few scraggly pieces here and there. Officer Miller had said Sarah still lived here. Looking around, it was hard to believe. I wondered if it were possible that the trauma of losing Chris had forced the family to take most of their belongings and stay with friends or something. But then why would Chris still be here? I had to know what was making that noise in the basement, no matter what the consequences.

As I walked around the rooms, I opened doors to see if there was anything that would help me piece this puzzle together. Still thinking of snarling, sneaky dogs, I was careful to peek around while still holding the doorknob so I could smash it shut if I needed to. Hey, it's no shame to be a chicken under these circumstances.

When I came to the kitchen, there was a door that was locked. Feeling sweat break out on my forehead, I rapped loudly on the door and listened for a reply. Instantly, the muffled sounds started up, this time with a thumping noise. I pictured Chris all wrapped up in a blanket thumping his head against the floor and yelling into a rag, trying to let me know he was there. Forgetting my fear, I looked around wildly for a key to unlock the door. I guessed that the door was locked more to keep him in than to keep me out, so I was hoping it would be somewhere close, rather than on a chain in the kidnapper's pocket.

I rummaged through the drawers holding stray silverware and pencils. Then, I saw a tray with assorted coins and nails and paperclips. And KEYS.

Chapter Seventeen

In my excitement, I pulled the drawer too far out and slammed the contents onto the floor with a loud crash. I clearly do not have a chance at being a career burglar. I didn't want to leave a big mess, partly because I'm a clean freak, and partly to erase any evidence that I had been there if I needed to hide, and partly because it was kind of embarrassing that I was being such a klutz. Ultimately I decided to toss the stuff back in the drawer and put it away in case someone came home while I was still there.

By now I was a nervous wreck, and my palms were sweating all over the keys in my hands. Why is it that when you are scared out of your senses your hands start getting the runs? You would think that dry palms would be more helpful in a frightening situation. I made a mental note to study about that later and try to find some purpose for having wet, clammy hands in a crisis.

Anyhoo, I went to the door with the keys and started putting them in the lock. The third key slid in smoothly, but it wouldn't turn. I tried jiggling it around for a few minutes, but it just wouldn't budge. I looked at the other keys in my hand for one that was similar. The rest were all too small or didn't have the right length. Thinking maybe it was still on the floor, I scanned the room with my eyes, which were slowly adjusting to the dark. There, in the corner, I saw a dark shape. When I walked over to it, I could see that it was a key. And it looked like the other one in my hand. Excitedly, I scooped it up and walked back over to the door. And then, I froze.

Someone was walking in the front door.

Chapter Eighteen

It's at times like these I wonder what Dr. Laurel would say to a person in my circumstances. I knew it was wrong to steal, but should I take the key with me? I knew it was wrong to sneak around in someone else's house, but would I have time to run across the house and out the door without being seen? Or heard? Or chopped into little pieces and fed to Rover the shredder? I had to decide, and decide NOW.

The safest thing seemed to be to take a chance and try to unlock the door in front of me. As quietly as possible, I slid the key into the lock, and it turned effortlessly and (thank goodness) soundlessly. I turned the knob and slipped inside the next room.

I had been so worried about the people coming in the door I had forgotten to consider what kind of room I might be entering. I had the good fortune of having not stepped too far over, because what was on the other side of the door was a staircase going down. It was pitch black, but I could feel the edge of the stair with my toe. As I ran my hand along the wall searching for a handrail or some kind of light switch, I felt a thick string of cobweb cling to my arm.

Do you know how hard it is not to make any noise when you are in a pitch black place and a cobweb touches your arm? Let me fill you in. All the movies you have ever seen about spiders as big as Wyoming hanging in the shadows of stairways fill your mind. It's true that I like spiders, but there is a qualifying difference: I CAN SEE THEM.

With as much stealth as possible, I pulled the web off my arm and gingerly made another attempt at finding a handrail. When I made contact with what seemed to be a piece of wood nailed to the wall, I slowly made my way down the stairs. I wondered if anyone was down at the bottom waiting to club me in the head. Not knowing what kind of people had come in the front door, or what lie below making those strange noises, I was having serious regrets about having come at all. I kept trying to focus on Chris and how scared he must be feeling.

When I felt the solidity of concrete beneath my feet I relaxed a little. At least I didn't have to worry about falling down the stairs anymore. While inching forward, I tried to forget Edgar Allen Poe's story about the Pit and the Pendulum. The damp smell of stale basement air accosted my nostrils. It felt cold and humid and I seriously wanted to find a light switch, even if it meant getting found out.

Remembering the possibility that I might not be alone, I whispered, "If there is someone else in here, make a very soft sound so I know where you are."

Immediately to my left there was a quiet bump. It sounded like a pillow had gently tapped the wall. Okay, so my roomie was apparently friendly. Hardly daring to move closer without further information about this person, I whispered, "Are you Chris?"

The response was a series of excited thumps that were loud enough to make me wish I could retract the question. It seemed clear that if this wasn't Chris, Thumper knew who he was. I took a deep breath (always a bad idea in such a stinky room) and walked over to where the noise was coming from.

Even though I was not walking quickly, my new friend was closer than I had anticipated, and I accidentally kicked him a little. I heard a sharp yipping sound, and suddenly my mind was flooded with images of all this trouble I had gone to just to find that a dog whose wagging tail sounds like a pillow hitting a wall was living in someone's basement. But the thing I kicked felt more like a person's leg than a dog's leg, so I got down on my hands and knees and started feeling around to get a better idea of what I was dealing with.

What I felt brought me both relief, and horror.

Chapter Nineteen

I felt a child's leg, but it was thick with some sort of slimy film. I didn't know if it was blood, mud, or if the child had been forced to use his pants as the bathroom. Being a sleuth, I probably should have raised my hand to my nose to learn more about the sticky substance, but hey, I'm not THAT gung ho of a detective.

I felt my way down the leg and discovered a rope tying the ankles together. It's not easy to untie someone when you can't see a thing, but after about twenty minutes of struggling and pulling, the knot began to slide apart and soon after the legs were free. I've watched enough spy movies to know that people who have their ankles tied together most probably have their wrists tied too, so I felt my way up and found the inevitable rope tying the hands. This one was not as tight, and came apart after about ten minutes of fumbling with it.

In retrospect I realize the first thing I should have done is see if there was something in the person's mouth, since there was no talking going on. I just thought we were both being quiet to keep the people upstairs from getting suspicious. After the hands and feet were free, the kid reached up and took something out of his mouth and gulped in some of the stale basement air. I guess it WOULD be hard to breathe with something shoved in your mouth like that.

Duh.

After he stopped gasping for air, he whispered, "How did you know it was me?"

Presuming he was referring to the fact that I had asked earlier if he were Chris, I very quietly told him I was the girl he had seen on the corner, when he was in the long gray car last month. I was about to explain further, but the people upstairs started making a lot of noise, and though it was hard to make out the words, it sounded like they were arguing. I remembered the people in the house next door that I had seen arguing and wondered if there was any kind of a connection at all. It sounded like there were two of them; a man and a woman.

Suddenly, there was a sound of breaking glass, a scream, and then a door slamming.

Chris and I didn't move a muscle for several minutes, even though the house was dead quiet. Maybe I should rephrase that. We were pretty scared to move, having only heard one person leave the house. Eventually, I got brave enough to whisper the basics of the story to Chris and he suggested we quietly go upstairs and see if we could escape. Even a run for it sounded better than staying down here in this stinky place.

Silently, we crept up the stairs.

Chapter Twenty

Remembering "the spider incident" I was careful to keep from touching the walls as we went upstairs. Every now and then one of us creaked a board, but it was so quiet upstairs I was beginning to wonder if both of them had left after all. The disturbing thought that there might have been more than two people crossed my mind, but I was trying to make myself feel better, not worse, so I kicked that thought to the curb.

At the top of the stairs I felt my hand shake as I grasped the familiar doorknob. Once opened, there was no turning back. I whispered to Chris, asking if he was ready, and he said, "I just have one question."

"What's that?" I breathed.

"What is your name?"

The question was so silly, so profound in its innocence, I

almost started laughing. Stifling my reaction, I simply told him my name and smiled at him in the darkness, even though he couldn't see it.

I steeled myself against the potential dangers and opened the door.

One thing I HADN'T been expecting was for it to be dark in the house. I must have been downstairs for quite a while, because the faint light that was in the room came from the stars that could be seen outside the window. Perfect. Under the cover of darkness we would be able to make our escape. Chris must have heard the gentle noise as soon as I did, because he forcefully tapped my shoulder without making a sound. We heard the distinct sound of someone snoring softly in the next room.

Chapter Twenty-One

I tried desperately to remember the layout of the house so we wouldn't bump into anything. Then, Chris tiptoed past me. Oh yeah—I had forgotten this was his house. He moved so quickly I had to move fast to keep up. When we got to the door he yanked it open, but the bad guys had a little surprise we hadn't anticipated. There was a chain fastened across the top. Not only did that stop the door from opening, it also made a terrible scraping, clanking noise that was sure to waken the snoring subjugator. There was a loud snort from the next room, and while Chris fumbled wildly to undo the chain, sleepy footsteps thundered down the hallway and into the kitchen. I was hoping the darkness would work to our advantage, but as Chris finally freed the door from the chain, a burst of light flooded the room.

The person standing with his hand on the switch was the same person I had seen wearing the chauffeur's uniform talking to the woman he had called Polly. As the door crashed open, I yelled, "SPLIT UP!" figuring it would be harder to find two moving targets in the dark than one. We both fled through the door and out into the night.

Though it was dark, I could see well enough to point to a large bush, and Chris, understanding my signal, dived behind it. I was hoping the man would see me running, and not look for Chris. Considering his legs had been tied up, he wouldn't have had a chance if it were a contest of who ran the fastest. After about a block and a half, I became concerned when I didn't hear footsteps running after me. I looked back and could see a person staggering after me in the far distance. Then, I remembered the breaking glass and the scream. I wondered if the captors had been drinking and the man had become drunk enough to pass out. It seemed a rational explanation, judging from the way he was weaving around while he tried to walk.

I had to act fast. I ran up to a house with the lights on and banged on the door. The woman who came to answer took a look at me and her mouth fell open. Not bothering to wait for an invitation, I pushed the door open and said, "I have to use the phone to call the police!" I'm usually a bit more polite, but I was afraid by looking at her that she was going to shut the door in my face, and I needed some help. She closed her mouth and just nodded her head as I picked up the phone and called 911.

Chapter Twenty-Two

It seemed to take an eternity for the police to get there. The staggering figure of the man chasing me got closer and closer as I paced the floor waiting. He seemed not to be able to tell where I went. My stomach tightened into a solid knot when he got close to the house, but then the chauffer kept on walking past it. I silently begged the lady not to make me go outside. She seemed content not to ask any questions, though I would have been firing questions at a kid banging on my door in the middle of the night wanting to call the police. Maybe she sensed my discomfort about discussing it. Whatever the reason, she watched me pace back and forth, until at last we saw the familiar black-and-white car through the plate glass window.

I ran out the door and looked around warily as my story

ricocheted around the quiet starlit night. While barking out what had happened, I was also looking for the man who had been chasing me, and found him just as he turned around the next block. I shouted for the police to go after him, and then ran in the opposite direction to go get Chris. Fortunately, I was making so little sense, one officer followed me. When I got to the bush, Chris was still under it. I could hear his teeth chattering 30 feet away, since he was only in a pair of shorts and a tee-shirt, with nothing on his feet at all. The officer and I both gasped when he stood in the light. His arms and legs were covered in blood from his attempt to free himself from the ropes. As the officer placed an arm around the boy, he collapsed into the man's side and burst into tears.

As we limped the poor kid into the squad car, the figure of a policeman walking with a man in handcuffs came into distant view. The last thing I remember was sitting down in the car. Suddenly, nothing had ever felt so good, and I fell fast asleep.

When the car stopped moving, we were in front of my house. I was quite surprised by this, as I couldn't remember telling the officer where I lived. Then I saw my parents rush out to the car and the realization flooded me that they must have been worried sick about where I was. I can be a rotten kid sometimes, but I'm punctual. When I wasn't home at curfew they must have freaked and called the police. Good ol' mom and dad.

Now that I was safe and sound, I had a burning curiosity to find out the answers to millions of questions. But I could tell it would have to wait until Chris had seen a doctor about his wounds.

The next day, I talked Delight's mom into taking Jennifer and Amanda to the hospital for their home school field trip. While they looked around and ate hospital cafeteria food, I paid a little visit to Chris in room 517.

This is the lowdown on what I learned:

He was on his way home from the park when his aunt Polly offered to give him a ride home. Seeing no harm in this, he let the chauffer put his bike in the trunk, and got in the car. Well, it seems aunt Polly wasn't doing so well financially, and thought it would be a slick trick to kidnap her own nephew and then "relay messages back and forth from the kidnapper." She even offered to stay at their rental home there in the same city in case she were needed. Apparently Chris' parents were really loaded, and she saw an opportunity to make a fortune. But then she and the chauffer started arguing over how much Chris should be ransomed for, so it was getting uglier and uglier for the poor kid while they fought about it.

"So that's why the police thought the address I gave them was your own house," I mused.

Chris rubbed his bandaged leg and sniffled a little. Then, he looked up at me.

"Thank you for not giving up," he said simply.

I thought about the many times I almost had. As I opened my mouth to speak, there was a knock at the door. A man looking to be about 40 years old had a huge basket of flowers in his arms. "DAD!" Chris yelled happily. He then proceeded to tell his father about the rescue. It sounded pretty cool the way he said it. I must admit it made me feel pretty heroic.

"There is the matter of a reward you know," his father said, turning to me. I had forgotten about it. Having been taught all my life to be humble, I wasn't sure what to say. I was going to refuse the money, but then visions of a tarantula terrarium filled my head, and I just said thank you when he placed the sealed envelope in my hand. Selfishly, I hoped it was at least 30 dollars so I could get one with a decent sized leg span. When Delight's mom asked me how my visit went, I patted the envelope in my pocket and just said, "Fine." I didn't dare open it until I got home.

I went straight to my room and locked my door. I didn't want anything to distract me from this moment. When I looked inside, my jaw dropped to the floor. There, in an envelope that was all mine, was a check for two thousand dollars!

SWEET!

Chapter Twenty-Three

Now that Chris is all healed, he is coming over to my house today. I told him I wanted him to take a look at what I bought with the reward money. I hope he likes spiders, because I got a huge hamster farm with tubes and wheels, and I bought 35 tarantulas to put in it.

Hey, a girl's gotta have a hobby!